To Eleanor,

Thanks for yo   u pport
and helping me to save my
website :)

Very best wishes

Ben Westwood

Welcome to

LEATHETON

by Ben Westwood

Contents

Foreword

by the author

Welcome to the first book of my poetry series –
'This is Leatheton'

As a new independent writer and publisher, your word-of-mouth is vital in getting others to discover this poetry series.

If there's anything in here that you particularly enjoy or connect with, or if you're a fan of the complete book – then you can let me and others know by writing your comments on social media with the hashtags '*#ThisIsLeatheton*' or '*#Leatheton*'.

You can also tag me on Twitter @PoemsFaRunaway

Despite being somewhat a work of fiction, Leatheton is not too far from most people's reality.
Most of these stories are inspired from somewhere, and one or two are mainly true.

Leatheton is the place that we all know.

Wholesome

All of those winter days and nights.
They would have been so lonely - without you.
Your beautiful smell, and your sweet taste.
You give me so much warmth.

You really do help keep me going,
Inspiring me to push through the day.
No time for feeling weak.
You give me power.
Oh yes you do.

I could never forget you.
And hardly a day goes by - when I don't think of you at
least once.
You know I've said this all before,
When we've both been there together,
As I place my hands around your vessel.

But I just want you to know that I really truly mean it.
I really do love you –
Porridge oats.
You're my favourite breakfast.

Love from
Frank.

13 Terrace Hill.

Adam the estate agent

"There's a train station just under a mile away,
and all the local amenities.
If you wanted to rent this place from tomorrow,
we could fill in the paperwork and sort out the keys."

The young couple that he was showing the two-
bedroomed flat to,
told him that they still weren't too sure.
"Come to think of it now that we've seen both of the
places,
we prefer the one that you showed us before."

"No worries" he replied, "We can sort that out today,
all I'd need is the seven-hundred pounds."
The lady then said "OK, we'll just need a few days,
to get the rest so I'll now ring around."

"No worries" said Adam "Would you like me to
drop you back off anywhere?"
"Oh that would be great, thanks a lot mate,
you could drop us back at your office please, yeah."

And so he dropped them off, and waved them goodbye,
went to his desk and then sat on the chair.
It was the end of the day and so he said to his colleague,
"I'm going to head off now then Claire."

His colleague then nodded whilst sorting her papers,
and so he then went to walk out of the door.
He then heard his boss shout "Can I please speak to you
Adam?"
He was on a warning and expecting one more.

And so Adam sat down in the seat of the office,
across the table from his boss called Ted.
"I gather that you've finally secured some tenants?"
Is then what Adam's boss said.

"I just need a few days, I've got two couples looking,
at the flats up on Brinsbyfield street."
His boss Ted shook his head and then went on and said,
"That's what you said to me last week."

"Don't take this personally, and I'm sorry to say,
but I don't think you're cut out for this stuff.
It hasn't been easy, but I've made a decision.
Please don't think that this one isn't tough."

Adam knew it was coming, "So you're firing me now?"
"I'm afraid so" then his boss Ted replied.
And so Adam got up whilst taking a breath,
and grabbed his coat that was folded by his side.

And so he then made his way, to the other side of town.
"Spare any change at all please there love?" asked Rose
the young beggar.
But he just walked on and kept his head down, as if he'd
not heard her at all.

"Ignorant twat" she then muttered on, loud enough so
that he could hear.
But all he could think of was that his fiancé was pregnant,
and she's due at the end of the year.

At least he'd already sorted the ring, which was in the
glove compartment inside of his car.
And that's where he went, to the multi-storey car park,
just a few hundred yards, not too far.
And so he walked up to level 4A, and looked where he'd
parked up before.
But all he could see was a now empty spot, and broken
glass down on the floor.

"Aaaarghghg" he screamed whilst kicking the floor, as if
things couldn't get any worse.
And that's when his phone had slipped out of his shirt
pocket, the screen cracked and it no longer works.

And so he then walked to the police station, now
frustrated and mind in a haze.
"We're really busy at the moment, but we've logged it all
in, you'll get a call back in a few days."

"But my wallet is inside that car, and my fiancé's wedding
ring too!"
"I'm sorry" replied the clerk behind the screen, "There's
nothing at all that I can do."

He walked out of there feeling like the whole world - was
collapsing in front of his eyes.

And so he then made his way back through the town, to
the taxi rank next to Shoewise.

Luckily Adam could just about remember his fiancé's
phone number from memory.
He'd call her and she could make sure that there'd be,
some money at home for a taxi.

And so he sought help from those that he saw in the town,
all he needed was to use a phone.
But the sequence of events had filled Adam with stress, all
he could think was to moan.

A somewhat frantic and panicky Adam, slightly unsure of
what he should do.
But everyone that he asked just walked on past, and said
"Sorry mate, I can't help you."

"Ee-aah mate" shouted the young beggar girl - still in the
doorway of the now empty town.
"You trying to score? And do you need a number? I can get
you a white or a brown."

"Nah" he replied, "Nothing like that. I'm stuck and I'm
trying to get home."
She then reached her arm into her coat pocket, and pulled
out a mobile phone.
"I've got some minutes on that, if you don't be too long,
even though you ignored me today."
He then thanked her a lot, and he truly said sorry, before
calling his fiancé.

"Hello there love, it's been a terrible day. I'll explain to you when I get back.
But in a nutshell, it's been my day from hell.
The car's been nicked and I've had the sack."

He then listens in as his fiancé asks questions, before Adam went on to then say –
"Is there thirty quid there, until I sort things out, if I get a taxi the whole way?"

After ending the call he then handed the phone, back to Rose whom was still sitting down.
And said he was sorry that he had nothing to give, but that he would next time he was in town.

"By any chance was your nicked car green?" she asked with a questioning glare.
The look in his eyes, then turned to surprise, as he then replied to the girl "yeah."

"I think I know who it was, because I saw it go past" she explained to Adam there with such ease.
He then pleaded "I'll give you a hundred quid, if you could help us get that car back, please?"

"Alright" she said and then pulled out her phone, went through her list and put the phone to her ear.
Adam was shocked at the intense and high volume that Rose shouted "listen up here!"

"You better tell Robbo to give my mate back his car, the green one that he's nicked from the town.

Because they know we've got stories, and I've kept quiet
too long, believe it they'll all get sent down."

"Ring him up now, and don't fuck about. And tell him
everything I've just said.
If word gets out what them blokes did to me, every one of
them will all soon be dead."

She then ends the call whilst Adam looks baffled, it starts
to rain and the pavement gets wet.
She moves her sleeping bag further into the doorway, and
said "That wrong-un deserves all that he gets."

Just a few minutes later her mobile rang, she spent a few
minutes there on the call.
"It's only just up the road, not far from the vets, but
they've driven it into a wall.
And if the ring they've cashed in was yours by any chance,
they've pawned it up by the bus station."
From that moment on, he knew he'd get it all back, an
instant release from his frustration.

He then made his way through the town to the vets, and
saw his car a few yards before.
The windows were smashed, but he'd got his car back, and
finally made his way home once more.

And on the next day he went to the pawn shop, and
explained that the ring there was his.
The police then got involved and in the end it was solved,
but he remembered that he gave a promise.

He couldn't really afford the whole hundred pounds, he
said to Rose that he could give.
But he got out a fifty to give it to her, and felt at least that
way he could live.

But he never did see Rose begging again, nor did they
cross paths in the street.
Until six years later he looked through a passing bus
window, and briefly saw her there sat on a seat.

Little Jack's mate

Mum's drunk again and god knows where dad is.
She don't listen to me when she's like this, always snaps
and so I think I'm better off out of the way.
But since we moved here to this little village, it seems
quiet here, and I'm mostly playing out on my own.

I'll be seven next year, old enough to play out a bit further
away, but now I'm going to the field over there by the big
tree.
Mum won't shout for me when she's like this, and I can go
and explore all the way over there by the stream.

And so I make my way up to the end of the garden, over
the stump and then through the long grass.
My shoes and socks are now soaking wet, but I'm getting
closer to the stream.
I hear the sound of crickets and the faint sound of water.
But what is all that splashing?
Not a giant fish is it?

As I get closer and step through the last bit of the long
grass,
I see a terrier with brown hair, in the middle of the stream.
He jumped out and launched at me, I'm scared that he
might bite.

I then fall on to the ground and hurt my elbow, whilst the
terrier licks my face.

I stand up as he looks up at me, his tongue is out whilst
he's panting and he's now wagging his tail.
His owner will be here in a moment no doubt,
"I can't believe you did that doggy!" I then said.

But how could I be angry, when he's smiling at me like
that?
"Alright then doggy" I said, whilst going to stroke his head.

But then he only goes and decides to shake off his dripping
wet coat, which splashes onto my face.
"Oh no doggy, don't do that next to me!"

But still no sight of a person he'd been walking with.
"Where's your owner?" I then asked.
But he's a dog isn't he, and of course he wasn't going to
answer me back, and all he did was look at me, and carry
on smiling whilst wagging his tail.

I'm going to try to skim some stones.
I've never really been able to do it.
Every time I throw one, the terrier barks and then
eventually my mum shouts me back in.

"Jaaaaaack! Jaaaaaaaack!" she shouts - and so I run back
towards the field.
"Bye doggy!" I shout, as I then make a run, but every step I
take the terrier is right behind me.

"Jaaaaaaack! Where are you Jack?" my mum calls.
"I'm coming Mum!" I shouted, whilst running back through
the long grass and to my garden fence.
I wasn't sure if she could even hear me, but I soon knew
that she had.

I then got back to our house, Mum is standing there, not
looking pleased.
She sees the terrier running behind me and then rushes
towards it.

"Shoo! Shoo! Get away!" she shouts.
"He's a nice dog Mum" I then say to her.
"Aaah you're right, he is actually" she then replied.
"Can we keep him? Pleeease?" I asked.

"I'm sorry love" my mum answered back, "He's someone
else's dog."

"His owner will be around no doubt, and we can't be
having a dog in the house.
Not with your new-born baby sister.
He'll be OK, just leave him be."

I knew that dog could understand a little bit.
Perhaps not the words exactly, but he tilted his head and
then let out a whine.

"Come in for your dinner Jack" said Mum.
And so I ate my ham and chips, sat at the kitchen table.

Not all of it though.

I'd ripped half of the ham off, and put it into my pocket
along with two roasted potatoes.
"Can I play out Mum? Pleeease?" I begged.
"OK" she replied, "But don't be bringing back any stray
dogs! And stay where I can see you!"
"OK Mum, thanks" I answered back, before darting out of
the back door.

There's no sign of any dog about, and so I run to the edge
of the field by our back gate, that has the giant uncut
grass.
All I can hear is the faint sound of wind blowing through it.
Then out of nowhere something is coming, and soon after
I can then hear him panting.

The terrier runs towards me with the same happy smile as
before, then sniffs inside my pocket before licking my face
again, and once more again then sniffs inside of my
pocket.

"These are for you doggy" I say, whilst pulling out the roast
potatoes and ham.
He dived in to them straight away, he's probably hungry by
now I thought.

It didn't take him long at all.
But then he jumped up and licked my face, and knocked
me back down again.
His smelly breath is horrible, but I still just can't help but
giggle from the tickling.
"Urgh!" I shout whilst laughing out, all I could hear was the
dog panting.
And so I got some sticks, and threw them for him to fetch.

I throw them as far as I can, sometimes too much until my
shoulder then hurt.
Every time he came running back, and dropped the stick
for me to throw again.

Time soon passed by, and Mum then shouted to call me in.
"Jaaaaaack! Jaaaaaack! Time to come in now."
And so I run back to our garden, whilst the little brown dog
whined at me again.

"Come on in now Jack. It's nearly your bedtime" Mum said
to me, not seeming as drunk as she had been before.
But what if that dog has got nowhere to go?
It's cold in the night, and it's not fair to just leave it out
there.

So before I make my way up the stairs - "Muuuum" I then
loudly shout.
"I've left my jumper at the end of the back garden by the
gate."

"Your jumpers here, I just moved it just now" Mum had
then replied.
"I had my other one there too" I said, hoping she didn't
know I'd lied.

"OK, go and get your jumper. But hurry up" she said.
And so I made my way to the end of the garden, and as
quietly as I could called out "Doggy! Ptssssst. Doggy!"

Still there in the grass he was, and then he made his way
towards me.

He then barked, "Shhh!" I said, as I sneaked us both
around the back of the shed.
I opened the door and moved all of dad's tools.
No-one would ever know, and it's warmer in here.
In the morning I'll bring him some more food and some
more water.

Mum's busy anyway, putting all the stuff away.
All she's to know is that I'm getting myself a cold drink.
If I'm really careful - I can use some towels from in the
cupboard,
for my new mate to sleep on.

Tomorrow was a Saturday, so there's plenty of time to let
him out.
I make him a bed, and leave a bowl of water.
He licks my face and wags his tail.
"See you mate" I say to him.
Before closing the shed door, and heading back inside.

When morning came I'd been awake not very long at all.
And then I heard Mum talking after someone had knocked
the door.
"Jaaaaack!" my mum then shouted, and so I ran down,
to see her standing with an old lady, that I'd not seen
before.

"Hello young sir" she said to me. "I've lost my dog called
Derry.
He's a little brown terrier. You haven't seen him anywhere
have you?"

"Yes, I think I saw him down by the garden. I think I might
know where he is" I said.
But I knew that I'd soon be in trouble if Mum knew that
he's inside of the shed.

"Well, if you can help me find my Derry, I'll give five
pounds to your mum for you" she said.
And so I replied that I'll try, and pretended that I,
had made my way to the top of the garden instead.

I snuck around the back of the shed,
And then I opened the door.
He darted right out and took a pee by the bush, before
then sprinting right through the house.

"There he is!" I heard the old lady say gleefully; at least
she's found her dog again now.
She thanked me greatly and said to Mum that I was a good
kid.
"Where did you find him?" she then asked me.
And so I said "Up there by the grass."

But at least I weren't in trouble, because no-one ever
knew,
that I'd made a bed inside the shed and kept him fed and
warm that night.
I'd got away with it all of my life.
Until I was sixteen years old, and my mum showed me her
old photos.

Shopkeeper Raj

Shopkeeper Raj, a local legend.
He knows where it's at.
He'll always welcome you, when you walk into his shop.

Even though he's had his windows smashed in twice,
he's still so nice to folk around.
And just last year he was in the local rag.

Not for handing out so much food on credit, or having his
sneaky lock-in's with the locals.
And not for the fun-run that he did that time when he
collapsed before he made it to the finish line.
But for the moment he risked his life, to save Becka
Mason's kitten.

It was exploring on the window ledge, jumped out and
then ran down,
to the road with passing traffic that was coming from up
town.
An approaching lorry's horn sounded, but the kitten didn't
flinch.
Raj jumped out into the road, and saved its life by half an
inch.

And every time that she now walks in to Raj's little shop,
they'll chat away as now their friends, at least five minutes
she will stop.

She's even got his number now inside of her phone.
And it's been a year since she's been racist - secretly at home.

Barry

I wake up in my shelter, open my eyes and lift up my head.
The sounds of the town's morning continue to play around
me.
I can hear buses go past, and a few people talking.

I shake the dust off of my bare feet, the dust that gathers
in this place that I sleep.
Sure I'm homeless , but that's just how it is.
I guess that I'm just free.

Not that I want a single persons sympathy, but there's
none here on this street anyway,
for someone like me, with a half-cocked eye and one a leg
that don't work.

I guess that it's time to hit the main street, somehow find
something to eat.
All I ate yesterday were a few bits of bread.
And I've got that starving feeling now in me.

It's eight forty-five in the morning.
I'll always get some food with so many people around.
And I don't worry about my pride, when people see me
inside of the bins.
One or two might look, but in general none of them ever
really notice me.

Sometimes I'll find a leftover sandwich, jump out of the
bin and get out of sight.
Thanking god for my blessings, whilst I take a bite.

Sometimes I just stand and eat it there on the street,
without a care in the world about what anyone thinks.
But I know really that it's better to be somewhere else,
when the people around just won't let me be.

They walk towards me like hawks, but at least I know that I
will survive.
Just no respect, it's nearly always me mainly moving for
them, even whilst I'm sat there eating.
Except for the few that still throw me something when
they see me around.

But I still always get by every day - and then I fly,
to the tower block that's just up the road.
I land on the windowsill of the old man with the plants.
He always feeds me and he's now named me Barry.

Mad Marcus

Mad Marcus was an old punk, that stood in Leatheton
Square,
near the side of the nightclub, he had spiked Mohawk hair.
But something made him different, from everyone one
else there,
He'd always dance to silent music, and have conversations
to the air.

Convinced of his reality, that was the world he lived.
People would come passing by on their night out, and
dance along in town with him.
Marcus jumped and danced and stomped, whilst trying to
speak.
Which often just was a strange sound, whilst flem came
spitting out from his mouth.

And every now and then he'd give a crazy beaming smile.
And look at you with so much love, someone really is in
there.
But then he's soon back talking - to the people in the air.

To some they may seem startled, when he got loud at
night.
But if you had knew Marcus, you knew that in his heart he
was alright.

People wave him a goodbye, when they have left the clubs.
But no one really knows, where Mad Marcus lives or sleeps.

Dedicated Caroline

Every day in Leatheton - an old lady walks by whilst
pushing her trolley,
Walking slow, and always with a woollen hat.
It's obvious her back is hunched, quite a lot in fact.
People often wonder where she always goes?
And does she have a family?

Not many see her turning off the road to Richard Street,
to be let inside of the squat that the old lady now lives at.
Among the youthful squatters, she's always warm and fed.
The end of the living room is draped off, where she now
has her bed.

She spends most of her days inside of the town library,
researching legal stuff all that she can.
To save Leatheton community centre, the only one that's
left around here, she's fighting hard to come up with a
plan.

She used to live around the corner, but she doesn't
anymore.
Because they've turned them into yuppy flats and kicked
out all of the poor.

She's now gathered a small army, of passionate recruits,
to come and join the worthy cause and put on their war
boots.

For a while she was the only one, shouting on her own.
But after over four years of dedication, the fruits of her
labour have shown.

As well as direct action, such as being locked to the gates,
they stayed and fought and went through court, and in the
end had won the case.
For five more years the centre stayed, before they had
pulled it to the ground,
simply because there never was, another Caroline around.

Jimmy-Jean the busker

Jimmy-Jean, he's the town's most famous busker.
He plays his music on the street.
Loved every moment that he played,
oh did Jimmy-Jean.

All the people of Leatheton loved his music,
but sometimes not one stall-holder,
whom seemed to see it as a threat,
and wanted to put an end to it.

But Jimmy-Jean he weren't no mug, he was tired of being
moved on by those that wouldn't share the street.
He said he wouldn't play too long, and that the other
traders didn't mind.
"Come on mate, I'll play just for an hour."

But that one stall-holder just wasn't having any of it.
"How am I supposed to sell all of my towels, with you
there playing your guitar?"

No-one else had seen the logic of the bitter stall-holder,
but they couldn't stop him calling the police on Jimmy-
Jean.

But Jimmy-Jean he didn't move, he'd had enough of being
degraded,
when all he really wanted was to practise his blues music.

Two policemen then came and seemed to take the side of the stall holder.
But Jimmy-Jean refused to move until he'd played for half an hour.

One policeman then said that if he didn't move, Jimmy-Jean would be arrested.
"Pack up your stuff and just move on, and don't cause us a stress."

But Jimmy-Jean the busker said "Look mate, this ain't fair on me.
I haven't even played a full song yet, come on I'm sixty-three."

"At least please let me make enough, to pay my fare home on my bus."
But one policeman there then replied "Please don't make a big fuss."

"We'll have to take you to the police car, if you won't move yourself."
Two policemen then took Jimmy's arm, one each side and sat him down inside the car, then locked him in and gathered up his stuff.

They both then went back to the car, and Jimmy-Jean was on his phone.
"Why's he taking pictures?" one officer then asked.

"I dunno, silly old bat.
Just let him get on with it. What can he do?"

They both then got in, and drove off towards the station.

"Why were you taking photographs mate?" the officer in
the passenger seat asked Jimmy-Jean.

"I wasn't taking photo's pal, since eleven thirty-five,
I've been streaming every bit of this, up on Facebook Live.
I've only got two hundred fans, but I can't believe this
mate -
That the amount of people watching this is four-thousand
two-hundred and sixty-eight.

"You should really read what they are saying mate,
I don't think that they're your fans.
There's people saying they are coming to town, driving in
their vans."

"How many people liked that comment?" one cop then
asked Jimmy-Jean.
"I don't know how to say this mate, but two hundred and
sixteen!"

The officers then briefly looked into each other's eyes.
Some sort of silent language that Jimmy-Jean didn't
understand.
The officer driving then shook his head.
"Take him back home" he then said.

They carried his stuff right to his door, and one officer
pulled out twenty pounds and gave it Jimmy-Jean, before
apologising.
But after that, when he went back, no-one ever bothered
Jimmy-Jean there once again.

(In memory of Johnny Walker 1980-2018)

Jimmy Jean

Big John's 'out there' moment

Big John for sure weren't no small fella.
Six-feet-six and built like bricks.
And it's now his Monday off,
from all of his weekend shifts.

Big John, he does the doors at the nightclub at Leatheton -
the nearest town.
On the weekend there is often trouble, but Big John can
sort it out.

But now he's put in this week's shifts, and got back to his
life.
He don't go to sleep yet, until he's seen his child and wife.

When his five year-old daughter Ella hears him, she comes
running down.
Always leaps into his arms, then he swings her around.
This morning he's made breakfast, his wife Katie is still
upstairs.
She's putting on her make up, and she's doing up her hair.

"Ring Ring" his daughter says. "Ring ring" she says again.
And he repeats it with a banana - as if it were a phone.

"Hello, who's there?" he says enthusiastically,
But Ella climbs down off her chair and goes into the living
room to get her own toy phone.

She's nattering away again, to her imaginary friend.
Big John he laughs as this moment has warmed him up
inside.

Ella seems as if she's listening, and answering back too.
"Yeah?.............Yeah?" before gasping.

Big John mutters to himself - "You've got that off your
mother you have."
As he stood stirring Ella's porridge, she walked back in with
her toy phone.

"OK" she said down the red toy handset - and held it up to
Big John.
"You Daddy, you Daddy" she said whilst waiting for him to
take it from her.
How could he not play along, it's what they always do.

"Hello? Who's this?" he said, about to wait a moment to
then say something again.
Then right out of nowhere, a woman's voice as clear as
light,
said "Don't go to work tomorrow night."
'Hold on' he thought, 'am I holding the house phone?'

He pulled it away from his ear to look at it again,
but all he had been holding was Ella's pretend plastic
phone.

It baffled him as he then looked at little Ella, whom grabbed the phone and then ran back into the living room and put it back down there.

'Surely it's just tiredness' Big john had then thought to himself.
"Everyone will think I'm mad, there's no-one I can tell."

It had bugged him all day and had bugged him all night, does he listen to that voice or not.
Or is he just mad? And is it sad, that he's even still thinking about it?

A Tuesday night at the nightclub he worked, weren't often very full to be fair.
So he rang up his workmates and he called in sick, and made sure that they had someone else there.
Kept checking the locks at home on every door, he'd pumped himself up for a possible fight.
And every few seconds was checking on Ella, to make sure that she was alright.

Big John is now in deep regret, "Is it something about work?"
"Should I have been there instead, in the case that something has gone down?"
"I'd better call the lads up" he then said to himself.

"Is everything alright there?" he asks.
"Yeah fine John" answers his colleague Martin.

"Just the usual Tuesday lot, nothing here to worry about.
Why are you asking by the way? And get well soon Big
John."

"Oh, just making sure that you've got people there to
cover.
Don't be afraid to call us if you really need to" Big John
responded back.

There's no way he wanted to raise alarm, from some
strange mad mental-health moment.
Martin had sounded a little confused as to why Big John
had seemed so concerned, but didn't really seem to think
too much of it at all.

"One second" said Martin before Big John overheard the
sounds of the nightclub over the line.
*"Oi you….no him…Oi! Don't fuckin pretend you can't hear
me, move the fuck away from there!"*

"Look John. I gotta go, speak to you later mate, get well
soon" Martin then said.
"Yeah, goodnight" Big John replied, before putting his
phone down on sofa where he was sat.

Every time he heard a car drive by, he'd taken notice of
the voice he'd heard, and took it as a sign.
Are con-men in the area? Or could there be a burglary?

The voice that told him not to go, was simply too strange
for Big John to ignore.
So he stayed at home and built a dolls house with Ella on
the floor.

But twenty-something minutes in, Ella then had changed
her plans.
She's now pulled out the big orange box with plastic
shapes and sand.

And then suddenly one moment, he hears a lady shout
outside.
"Please someone help me, my poor Derry has got stuck!"

"What's the matter love?" he calls to her, whilst standing
at his door.
The old lady then came troddling over.
"It's my Derry again, he tried to chase a rat,
and now he's got himself stuck, in that bit of old piping."

Big John then walked over, whilst pulling on Derry's collar
lead.
But it's no use.
Derry's only gone and got himself stuck yet again.

Derry yelped as Big John tried to pull him out of there
some more.
"I'm sorry love, he's proper stuck. Do you want me to get
the saw?"
"If that's OK" she then replied "Thank you oh so much,
you're so kind."
"I'll be a sec, one moment love" said Big John, before
going back inside.

A minute later he was back, with a hacksaw in his hand.
Derry whined whilst stuck inside, he won't be so fast to
chase rats through pipes the next time.

And just a few minutes later, Big John broke the pipe open,
and Derry was once again free.

And it turned out that from that moment Big John's
evening went perfectly alright.
Another story to tell the lads, on his return on the next
night.

Sergeant Walter

Sometimes on the streets of Leatheton, you will see a
man.
His name is Walter and he stands tall and proud,
whilst walking through the Leatheton streets still in his old
army uniform.
He gets respect from his days serving for his country.

He's done it all, yes Walter has.
Jumped out of planes, rescue missions and once even
saved a village.
But don't probe and ask him too much because he's got
Post-Traumatic-Stress-Disorder.

But he'll still tell you what he wants you to hear,
whilst reminiscing of the times he spent serving for his
country.

He still presses his uniform, all proper and clean.
And he'll show you all of the medals he's earnt,
whilst explaining quite graphically of how a bomb
exploded near him, and how he saw his friends get
burned.
Enough to startle anyone.

And that's when you see how much Walter's been
affected by so many tragedies.
And you just can't help but feel sorry for him, and show
him some respect and sympathy.

But one day in Leatheton when Walter was in town,
it seemed there was some kind of trouble and something
was going down.
Two men then approached him, and asked why he was
wearing his uniform whilst walking around.

"What regiment were you in then?" one man had then
asked.
So Walter then to them explained, in what seemed quite
some detail,
And his story did seem somewhat credible, to an untrained
eye.

.

Walter protested the two men's questions, pleading and
asking why.
Claiming that he wouldn't lie,
and that they should mind their own business – and leave
him the heck alone.

But there was nothing at all that he could say,
to now hide the fact that he's not once ever done a day,
serving in the army.
His stories were a fantasy, that not everyone had
questioned.
As for his medals and his uniforms - everything's from
eBay.

When little Jack ran off

It hadn't been so obvious to the little lad called Jack,
that his Dad wasn't really away working, and that he
wasn't coming back.
And on one night when his mum seemed angry, he
thought that he should be out of the way.
There was the playpark down in Leatheton, where he
could live and stay.

Out of the rain, and he could play for as long as he liked.
Just get away for a day, give his mum some needed space,
and he'll come back again maybe tomorrow.

It's not fair anyway, Mum and Dad stay out sometimes,
why can't I too either?
I shouldn't be in trouble, if they both do it too.
And besides, I'm not a small kid any more, I'm nearly seven
years old now.

I'll say that I've slept at my friend Noah's house.
It will be alright.
I better now try to sneak out whilst Mum is there on
Facebook, and now whilst I'm out of sight.

To the end of the back garden I go, and through the grass
back to the stream.
There's not as much water flowing through there as the
last few times I was here.

It makes it a lot easier to step through without getting wet.

Along the field's footpaths little Jack then walked,
until he then got to a road.
He thought this road led into town if he had just walked
straight down.
But he'd forgotten of one turning that people had to take.

And so after walking for over half an hour, he then found
himself in the village of Willsbury Green.

A bus had stopped along in front of him.
School children from the high school in Leatheton were
inside, wearing their black blazers.
They then all got off the bus.

One young lad then chases his friend and puts him in a
headlock.
Three young girls they all link arms, and walk off up the
road.

Little Jack keeps walking, past the two twelve year olds
with vaporisers in their hands and the cloud of synthetic
smelling Bakewell tart vapour that is in the air.

"I think I'm lost, which way's Leatheton?" asked little Jack.
"That way" replied one of the boys whilst pointing with his
vaporiser down the road, in the direction that the bus had
just arrived from.

The schoolboy didn't seem to realise that Jack was going to walk the four miles there, or really think about why he was asking.
Jack didn't know how far it really was, he'd never walked it to Leatheton before, but he knew it wasn't far.

By now his mum had noticed that he was not at home, checked outside and walked around and panicked.
She's running down the back fields now, on her phone to the police.
"I've lost my seven year old son, oh my god! Oh no! Please help me! Please!"

She ran along the footpaths whilst shouting out her cries.
But little Jack is now two and a half miles away as the crow flies.
The local police are out there looking in all of the places that come to mind.
"Don't panic love" said one PC,
"You're little son we'll find."

"Please, I bloody hope so" she said with great concern, before releasing a much needed breath, then drops her head into her hands.

The news quickly spreads around the village.
Now concerned neighbours drive around, whilst looking out for little Jack.

Everyone's checked all of the parks, except for the one that little Jack was at.

The little place in Gedely village, outside of the library that nobody really goes to, except for maybe one or two.

A tiny place, and not that many people even drive through there.

Little Jack then soon got bored and left the park to carry on to Leatheton.
And when he'd walked a mile away, he noticed something on the floor.
It was a muddy, dirty old twenty pound note, at least he thought it did look real.
'I'm sure that's not a toy one, it looks quite good to me.'

As he got closer to Leatheton town, he walked into a newsagents, and brought himself a gobstopper and a can of ice-cream soda.

'I've still got nineteen pounds left here, I can do anything, what should I do?
I'll head to the bus station and find a place to go.'

He ended up in Leatheton in no time at all, and discovered the train station, and for some reason the barriers were open.
He made his way onto a platform where soon there was a train.

Jack got on and then sat down, and the train doors then closed after him.
The train had then pulled away and then one moment later,

Jack heard a voice say from behind "Tickets, passes please."

"Where are you going young man?" the ticket man asked little Jack.
"Alton Towers train station" little Jack had answered back.
"And who are you going all the way there with? And where are your parents mate?"
"Oh my Uncle Steve" then Jack replied, "But he'll meet me there as he is late."

"And who's then got your ticket?" the ticket man asked little Jack.
"I've got my own money" little Jack replied.

"I tell you what kid, I'll do you a favour, this ticket here you don't have to pay for, and it'll take you the next two stops. My ticket machine is broken right now, but if you knock on the end carriage door over there, I'll write you a ticket that will get you all the way to Alton Towers mate, yeah?"

"Thanks a lot" replied little Jack, excited that he was now on his adventure.
The ticket man came past again shortly after.
"Dilton Parkway is the next station mate. Remember to knock on my door when it gets there and I'll give you the ticket.
It won't cost you anything then" the ticket man said whilst walking towards his door.

"Alright mate. Thanks" replied little Jack, now dreaming of the rides and what was there to see.

He'd never been before, but had seen it on the TV.

Six minutes later another announcement is made over the tannoy.

"Ladies and Gentleman, we are now approaching Dilton Parkway.
Dilton Parkway is our next station stop.
For those alighting, please make sure that you've got all of your luggage and belongings with you.
Dilton Parkway is the next station stop."

Jack looked at the door the ticket man was sat behind, so as to wait to get another ticket.
The train then stopped along the platform, at Dilton Parkway station.

On the train got on two women police officers, with uniforms and hats.
"Aren't **you** a long way from home there young man.
Come on little Jack, your mum's been worried sick."

Mad Macka

Mad Macka lived on the Birchtree estate,
just down from the White Lion pub.
Every time he got paid his universal credit,
he'd only just had enough to pay his debts and get grub.

Mad Macka does crime, all of the time, if anyone knows
what's gone down it is him.
And if you've had something stolen and want to know
where it's at, it's always worth asking at Mad Macka's flat.

Mad Macka ain't the type to be stealing from shops, unless
he's done no other jobs,
like robbing local factories or he's found a dealers grow.

Never on his doorstep mind, and sometimes even he's
surprised to find that he had somehow got away with half
of his crimes.

And not all of those he hangs around, agrees with all that
Mad Macka does,
but he don't see no fuss in it, and life's too short for him.
But Mad Macka's getting on now, he ain't no spring
chicken any more,
and over the last five years, Mad Macka's been close to
getting caught.

Mad Macka smokes strong cannabis to try and help with
his bad back,
if he's not outside with all the neighbours in the cul-de-
sac.
But just last week the council came, and not because of
the rats.
Mad Macka's got an ASBO, the smoke was stinking out the
flats.

The last two weeks has brought attention, so Mad Macka
kept his head down.
Until he'd ran out of money, and went shoplifting in
Leatheton town.

Walked in a supermarket, the one next to the big bank.
Grabbed a carton of fresh juice, opened it, then drank.
Walked up to the meat fridge, and shoved packets down
his jeans,
before stealing seven chocolate bars, and two tins of
baked beans.

He made his way out of the shop, and he thought that he
was now free.
Until a younger man jumped in front of him, and said
"Please sir come with me."

Mad Macka was the type to run, and if he had to he would
push.
But today Mad Macka didn't, and on this occasion
admitted defeat,
And walked with the security man back inside of the shop.

Behind the staff door and then in to a back room,
Mad Macka pulled out everything that he had nicked.
"I'm sorry mate, you got me" said Mad Macka by the door,
to the security guard twenty years younger aged at thirty -
four.

"I'm just a bit hungry. What do I do? Eat from a bin?
I can barely just survive, since the bedroom tax came in."
Mad Macka then cheekily asked, that as he had walked so
far,
if the security guard would let him get away - with just
one chocolate bar.

"I'll tell you what" said the security, "I'm going have to ban
you mate,
but there might be some cold pastries, as it's getting late.
But I'm gonna have to take your name, and if you've no ID,
I'll have to call the police, or I'll get sacked, it's policy.

"I've only got a letter on me" said Mad Macka now with
stress.
"It should be fine I think mate ,if it has on your address."

Mad Macka opened up the letter, and then passed it the
guy.
"That's the only ID on me, but I swear it's not a lie."

"Seems official enough" said the security guy before
looking close at the name.

"Andrew McCarthy" he then muttered quietly, whilst
writing it down in his book.

But Mad Macka then noticed the guy in deep thought.
Was Mad Macka again going to once more get caught,
for other crimes that he thought that he'd got away from?

The security guy then looked back at Mad Macka's way,
looked in his eyes, before then going on to say -
"Are you a guy that people call Mad Macka?"

Mad Macka gave two answers.
One with his words and one with his eyes, feeling there
was now some rapport between the both of them.

"No, that's someone else" he said before winking with his
eye.
"I can't believe I'm saying this" replied the security guy.
"Well you've been caught but listen up, it isn't all that bad.
Let's go and find somewhere to eat, it's nice to meet you
Dad."

The time Leatheton got snowed in

Leatheton's roads have all iced over, and now there are no
trains.
The schools have all closed for today, so they say on the
local radio.

"For those of you stuck at home or in traffic" the presenter
enthusiastically says –
"Here is 'You're My Fire' by James Hinton and the
Pollinators."

Every now and then you'll see a snowman, and around one
in six,
some pranksters have placed a snow-nob, or a snow pair
of tits.
The kids on Gor Hill are all sledging, and the pubs today
are packed.
It seems they all love their day off, and everyone's relaxed.

The motley crew of squatters that have since moved
across the town,
to the old big cinema, that ten years ago closed down,
have made their way through local streets, half of them
with spades too,
to clear the ice off footpaths, so that the old people could
walk through.

Or mum's with prams that could soon slip, and so that
nobody breaks a bone.
And when the neighbours start to meet them,
the squatters bring them back to home.

All of the neighbours that came back to where the
squatters heads at night had laid,
were intrigued to see the cinema, for the first time in a
decade.
"I used come here as a teenager" an old lady had
explained.
"And when I was courting with my George, back in our
early days."

Four squatters and six neighbours, then all walked in
through the door.
It was much cleaner than expected, because the squatters
had cleaned it all.
Despite that builders had ripped out half of the stuff, and
the local kids had kept breaking in -
The squatters had painted much of the inside, and fixed up
almost everything.

And so for two months in the old picture-house,
the neighbours would all pop around.
And word had soon reached the community, that this
bunch there were sound.

And on the weekend when they had to leave the place
they'd been in since September -
there was the best party in quite some time,
that Leatheton could remember.

Don the champ

If you were to pass through Leatheton town on an early
afternoon,
and walk along the high street, you might just meet Don
the champ.
He paces up along the road between the pound-shop and
the jewellers.
Always with his top off, and sometimes sits on the same
bench, with an unplugged lamp.

But lamp or not you'd know it's Don,
on his waist you'll always see.
The belt he won when middleweight, in nineteen seventy-
three.
And although he's now past seventy, and none of his old
friends are about,
he'll say to big blokes "Think you're hard?" - and offer
people out.

And on a summers day in town, his belt glistens in the sun.
As he strides along the high street, showing off to
everyone.
That's he's the hardest guy around, no fight that he'll turn
down.
He puts the geezers in hysterics every time they are in
town.

He's famous in these parts is Don, for sure he will be missed,
when his time comes but people still make jokes and raise their fists.

Don is ready for a fight, does a stretch and clicks his neck -
Until the man that's there with Don, says to his mates "Oh what the heck?"

Don he tries to swing a punch, but he can't throw one any more.
Because just like the last time he did this, he fell down to the floor.

And once again they've helped him up, and Don then tells them "Thanks".
They then reply "No worries Don.
You take care there champ."

Celebrity status

Derry's only gone and got under the fence again.
And now he's ran off down the road and barks outside a chicken pen.
The woman in the grey stone house comes to grab his collar.
But Derry's having none of it, and runs down a garden path.

Right through their big back garden, he scares away their cats.
But Derry didn't notice them, he's headed for the grass.
And then he dropped on to the floor, it looked like Derry had a fit.
But he was having one great time, rolling around in shit.

He made his way then to the field, through a hole there in the fence.
He then looked up into the sky, and then saw something moving high.
Big and red and moving fast, and then Derry heard some voices.

A family in the field there, were flying their young son's new Kite, so Derry sprinted over.
So excited Derry was, tongue was out and tail wagged at the thought of some new friends.

"Ah, hello you happy thing" the young boys Mum then said
to Derry.
As she bent down he placed his paws there on her knees
and barked.

But for some unknown reason to everybody else,
it seemed that Derry maybe wanted this whole field to
himself.
He got angry with the woman, his barks then had turned
to growls.
The dad then moved towards Derry, "Get the heck away!"
he scowled.

But Derry then chased the young boy, whom thought that
it was maybe because of his kite.
Both the young boy and his little sister, ran off out of sight.

The kids mum had then ran over to them - their dad then
gathered up all of their stuff.
Derry then moved his head down, and continued to growl,
and as the dad left - Derry went "Ruff! Rrrrrr. Ruff!"

Then as the dad had got away, he then turned around to
look.
And saw two trees were quickly falling down.

The trees were sinking from where they had been
standing, and the land had now started to slide.

Faintly in the distance, they could hear Derry's cries.

It was another Leatheton sinkhole, and in just two years in
this town there were five.
They've been lucky so far, when one swallowed a car,
when the land fell in on an old mine.

The dad then ran off over, after telling his family to stay
where they were.
"Wow!" he shouted, whilst walking further –
"Oh my freakin god!"

The land was now completely caved in at least twenty-five
feet squared.
He then looked down to see if he could see Derry there
anywhere.
"Is there something down there moving?" the father
muttered to himself.
Derry whines, he's trapped again, and needs someone to
help.

"Don't worry mate we'll get you out" the dad then said
down to Derry.
He paced around for a phone signal, but he could not get
any.
They drove a minute down the road, and then called the
police and fire brigade,
and whilst explaining everything, that's when it had then
hit them.

The father he then looked amazed, as he turned around
and looked deep into the eyes of his wife.

"That little brown dog that was barking at us, I think has just gone and saved all of our lives."

They drove back to the field and waited for some help.
Ten minutes later help had arrived, fourteen folk in all.
Two fire engines had turned up, and three cars full of police.
Little Derry is in panic now, slipping further down.

The sinkhole's not safe to be around, two men almost fall in.
The drop is at least twenty-five feet, and not all attempts are working.
After one long hour has passed, the press have now arrived.
It's now going live and national, of how this dog has saved their lives.

"Do you know who owns this dog?" the news reporters ask.
Up and down the country, everyone's now watching the dog that barked and saved all of the family.
They describe Derry pretty well, and make a point of his red collar.
His owner stirs a cup of tea, then see's the scene on the TV, before calling out "Oh Derry!"

By seven o'clock in the evening, it seemed that panic had started to grow.
What will happen when it gets too dark?
Can we get this dog out, we really don't know.

By now Derry's owner has arrived at the scene - sat in the
front of a police car, with a steaming cup of tea.
The sun is now starting to set, and it seems they are no
closer yet.
But up and down the country, everyone's now saying -
"Pray for Derry."

The news cameras still show some of the scene, but they
are not allowed too close.
Bright lights are dangled down with rope, so that the
rescuers can see.

Some of the folk, had lost some hope –
as they close their lips together, and prepare for the worst.

"Whoa, Whoa, Whoa" call out three voices, all at the same
time.
Everybody turned.
What's now going on?

The camera crews and news reporters all then went to run
up the field.
A policeman and policewoman then jump into their way.
"We've told you before, it's really not safe!"
And behind them they then heard a big cheer.

Just a few moments later a camera zooms in, to a
firefighter holding up Derry.
They've now got off all of the mud, from inside of his
mouth, that had nearly stopped him from breathing.

And once they've given him some water, and wrapped
Derry up with a blanket,
they took Derry back to the police car.

Numerous folk from the press are following every next
step,
as his owner calls out "Oh Derry! There you are!"

"How does it feel to be reunited with Derry?"
A female news reporter asks whilst holding a microphone.

*"I just want to thank everyone that's helped, they can all
come round to mine whenever they like.
They'll always be biscuits and tea brewing for them, I don't
know how I could ever repay them.
Derry means the world to me, and I thank them very
much."*

The news reporter humbly smiles.
"Is that just an excuse to have all those firefighters in your
living room is it?" the news reporter jokes.
"Not at my age" replied Derry's owner, *"I'd have them in
my bedroom."*

The news reporter bursts out laughing "Well that's it then"
she says whilst looking into the camera.
"Derry the dog is now confirmed safe and well.
Over to Shannon and the rest of the team."

Over in a London pub, as there had been no game -
five men that were drinking whilst the news was on, had
chanted Derry's name.

And inside of many households, through the whole
country that night,
at least a million people had seen him safe and said how it
was nice.

The next day his owners doorbell, had kept on being
pressed non-stop.
So many people from Leatheton and beyond had now
gone to see Derry.
By six o'clock the day was long, so his owner said -
*"You can all see him again tomorrow, but please come
back then instead.*

Derry needs some rest right now, and I think that I do too."
She counted those waiting in the morning, no less than
twenty two.

Now everywhere that Derry goes, he's a dog that everyone
knows.
They stop to pat him and say hello.
He's famous now around here.

Facebook memes and Instagram -
selfies every week.
And when his owner sometimes checks the post, she'll find
there's some dog treats.

The Leatheton sightings

On one summer morning, a retired farmer walked his
German Shepherd,
in the village, half a mile from the local shop.

He then turned off the roadside, and walked up to another
farmer's gate.
He pushed it open, the dog walked through - and ran up to
the top.

As the man walked through the field, he looked around to
his right,
and started getting curious at the sudden sight.

A group of people were in the wheat field, cameras by
their sides.
Had there been another murder? Or another suicide?

But there hadn't been a cordon there, and he hadn't seen
any police.
And so he walked on over, whilst his dog was by the trees.

"What's happened here?" the retired farmer asked, and
then the men had turned around.
"Crop circles" one man answered back, "There are two
near here we've found."

"It's probably merry pranksters" the retired farmer then
replied.

One bloke then said "They couldn't of, even if they tried."

"These patterns here done overnight, would be really too
complex.
And the way the wheat is crossing down, we've not ever
seen once yet."

"And what is it all that you lot do?" the retired farmer
asked.
"Are you some of those lot that look for the aliens? UFO
enthusiasts?"

"Well those two there are, but not me myself" said a man
holding a leather brown clipboard.
"My name is Phil Andrews from the Leatheton Gazette,
and this is what I've been sent to report."

And then by midday, it was posted all over Facebook,
on the Leatheton Gazette's main news website.
And on the next day, the story went national,
it was in every newspaper in sight.

Hordes of people from across the country came travelling
to Leatheton town.
There were vans full of hippies sharing internet
conspiracies,
and it spread quite a big buzz around.

There were one or two parties up on Omalley Hill,
and the locals had got it on the fun.
Until five crop circles appeared not far from Stonehenge,
and then suddenly in the town there was no-one.

An interesting week for a town like Leatheton, and it was
one to remember for sure.
We've got our local legends, and historic stories, but never
UFO's here before.

The chief editor of the Leatheton Gazzette,
two weeks later then received a call,
from a man named Clement Scott, that ran a firm called
'PR-all'.
"It worked so well!" Clement had said, "It's really all gone
down a treat.
We need another three making this time next week -
Can you please ask again 'Crop Circle Pete'?"

Oh no not Becky Manning!

"Oh no not Becky Manning!" often people say,
whenever there's a local serious emergency.
We've had yet another sinkhole, and a young lad that had
got trapped.
Becky's only gone and brought her dog again, and all it did
was yap.

The fire crew and local police said "Put it on its lead!"
And she replied "But my dog Ralph, could save that boy in
need!"

"Stop turning up at these things Becky! Last time did I not
say?
When my colleague fell and broke his leg, and the robber
got away?
Sure he'd ran on to the roof, but it was all going well.
Until you brought that little dog, and then our ladder fell."

"And what about the time before?
When there was a fire in the office buildings in town.
Letting off your own dog to go and find all the people,
it ain't the way that things go down."

"He could have got trapped. Are you listening Becky?
I hope you are, because this ain't no joke.

He's really quite tiny and wouldn't last five minutes,
breathing in thick dirty smoke."

"If it's any conciliation, you're not the only one,
that's desperate to be a celebrity.
There's three of you in town, that all bring your pets down,
trying to get your dogs on the TV."

Leatheton folklore

Our old town of Leatheton, we all know the stories.
And no-one really questions if they are really true.
Crop circles and our Derry, is all our town is famous for,
except for a few more stories, of Leatheton folklore.

The most haunted place in Leatheton, they say is at the
Potter's Wheel Inn.
Everyone that's had a room in there, seemed to have a
strange feeling.
There's been folk say that they saw a ghost, at the end of
the hallway -
Dragging across what seems like - a bag of heavy clay.

We've got the haunted train tunnel, where the kids say
someone died.
No-one knows where the story ever came from, and it
simply isn't true.

And then we've got old Billy Gray, they say he walks
through town at night.
Past the barbers and the market square, and then he turns
a right.

To where used to be his old farmhouse, back in 1623.
Before they hung him in the square, for a conspiracy.
They say the ghost of Billy Gray, will launch towards big
groups.
But if you shout "Billy" three times, he then will run away.

And then we've got St Richard's Road, they say there is
one part.
Where people see a horse and carriage, when it's after
dark.
Some people said they'd driven past, and thought some
Romany's were stuck.
And said they then turned right around, to go and take a
look.
And although it seemed no time at all, it raised up all their
hair,
To see that when they'd gone to help, that nobody was
there.

I'm sure there'll be new stories, of Leatheton folklaw.
Because the one's that I've just told you, no-one tells them
anymore.

Cattlemarket Lane

Cattlemarket Lane in town, ain't the place it used to be.
It seems that what from I remember, everything has gone.
Mark the guy that cuts our keys and Gerry the greengrocer,
the butchers shop and hardware store have packed up and moved on.

The winding lane seems empty now, most of the shops are closed.
All that's there are two vape-pen shops, and a place that gives out loans.
Two betting shops, there's one each side, across from one another.
And a crack addict shouts up the road, to her supposed lover.

Where once stood the big post office, now remains a mystery.
It hasn't been anything for ages now, for years it's been left empty.
The street has lost its buzz and feeling, and now the only bit that's nice,
is at the end towards the park, near the Citizen's Advice.

It's now the go-to spot for dealers, and now there's two girls on the game.
It ain't the way it used to be, on Cattlemarket Lane.

Gorgeous Kate

All of the men that pass through town, admire Gorgeous
Kate.
And she don't have to try a lot, it's just the way she is.
Every bar that she goes to, men offer her a pint.
But she's the type to often say "No thank you, I'm alright."

Some drunken lads will try their best, to come up with a
plan.
Even though that plenty know that she's got another man.
But Gorgeous Kate don't roll like that, and so they soon all
learn,
that being close to Gorgeous Kate, is something they'll
have to earn.

Gorgeous Kate does topless modelling,
and models for catalogues selling cheap women's clothes.
She'll always gets people's attention,
and it's obvious that Gorgeous Kate knows.

She could have any man she wanted, that she chose there
on the street,
it's not only the way she looks, the way she acts is sweet.
Her boyfriend has got severe brain damage, his bike was
smashed up from the rear.
And now he's soon to be her fiancé, she's marrying him
next year.

Peter the Big Issue man

Peter the Big Issue man, stands outside the supermarket,
every other day.
He's been here almost twenty years -
On the weekend he might have beers, but he don't do
drugs at all.

He's the man that people seem to go to and ask all of their
questions,
such as what time all shops will close, and detailed
directions.

He used to be the only one that sold the Big Issue here,
but since last year he shares the town with one girl from
Romania.
She stands at the other side of town, and sometimes
brings him cups of tea.
When they first met they both argued, but they now look
out for one another.

Sometimes Peter comes to town, on a Friday or a Saturday
night,
when people have been drinking beers, Peter then will do
alright.
On a good night he might make enough, to last him a
whole week,
when women hand him five-pound notes, and kiss him on
the cheek.

In the daytime people greet him, as they pass through town.
He's often the first one to be there and help, when an old person seems to be stopping.

He'll carry their bags to the taxi rank, and accepts no tips from them at all.
And without our Peter outside the supermarket, you'd just be looking at a brick wall.

Mario's

One night in Mario's kebab shop, there were just two folk
eating in.
Mario was behind the counter, watching the TV.
All of a sudden he leaped right up, and yelled right out like
crazy.

"Yeeeessss!" he shouted around three times,
"Oh thank you god!" once again out loud.
He passed the diners twenty quid and said –
"The foods on me."

He'd matched five numbers and the bonus, and won
himself a million.
The Leatheton Gazette turned up the next day, to run
another feature.

He had a party in the shop that week, the food was all on
him.
Mario's had been jam packed, but all were welcome in.

And even though Mario, still has six hundred grand.
You'll still find him behind the counter, with food tongues
in his hand.

Everyone knows Mario, and they think that he's sound.
He'll give for free if you are homeless, and if you're rich
just charge three pounds.

The week the gypsies came to town.

Two Romany caravans and one horse-drawn carriage,
had turned up on one hot august night.
It wasn't long until all of Leatheton knew,
of what in this town is a rare sight.

The gypsies were parked on the old youth centre's fields,
that no-one has really used much for years.
But over on Facebook's 'We Love Leatheton' page,
some people were expressing their fears.

"The last time that we had travellers come to this town,
half of the park had got trashed."
The neighbours were angry and so launched a vendetta,
and it led to the gypsies being harassed.

But not all of the people in Leatheton are like that,
on the page a woman called Steph was concerned.
She went and spoke to one gypsy, to give them a warning,
of what she had recently heard.

"Be careful" she said, "they've said all sorts of things,
And ways to try and make you all leave."
"Don't worry" he said, "Look at me, am I dead?
I've got stories that you wouldn't believe."

She'd stopped and had three teas with them, and chatted
for two hours.
She helped the gypsies move their things, when all of a
sudden came showers.
She then got home somewhat refreshed, from a different
day,
and logged back on to Facebook, with plenty more to say.

It was a valuable opinion, "They seemed quite nice" she
had typed in.
"Everything was looking clean, all of their rubbish in the
bin.
They said they'll only stop two days, no need to lock your
homes.
But can we stop the local kids, that keep on throwing
stones?

And two days later, as they'd said, before the council had
come down.
They had moved on, that was the week the gypsies came
to town.

Young rebel

Charlie Taylor was a lad, of fifteen years old.
Deep down was a kind-hearted kid, but never did as he
was told.
Not for no reason, Charlie Taylor always gave thought for
good.
But in a place with little hope, he felt misunderstood.

Charlie Taylor he lived up on the Birchtree estate.
Where the only pub within a mile, was soon to see its fate.
Charlie Taylor practised calm, and so he took to task,
to save his family memories, and a piece of Leatheton's
past.

"What about the old miners, that still come in here to
chat?
And Helga the old Swedish woman, that brings along her
cat.
How will Saturday nights around here ever be the same?
Will we all have to go all the way down town, if we want to
watch a game?"

He wrote to the pub company, whom seemed to laugh it
off.
Just a kid, only fifteen, there's nothing he will do.

And so he wrote to everyone, including his MP.
To his surprise they popped along, with the community.

Charlie passed flyers to folk in town, and lots of people got
involved.
Some said they'd help him save the pub, and some simply
just wished him good luck.

And on the day they were due to close down,
Birchtree Estate Working Men's Club.
All the neighbours were there, with big signs in the air,
And Mario had supplied all of the grub.

They all signed the petition, and so came the press,
from the local Leatheton Gazette.
It's all been postponed now, until late next year,
they ain't taken our old local just yet.

Leatheton United

One Tuesday in early September,
Half a mile from the Birchtree Estate,
a group of men were doing their football training,
after work and it was now getting late.

We've got Don Rae the scruffy painter, whom doesn't do
too bad in goal.
Although he often saves the ball, we've been on a bad roll.

We've got Jim Barr the electrician, right-centre mid, can
strike a ball.
Francis Robinson in left-central defence, at six-foot-six-
inches tall.

We've got Clive Clarke in left midfield,
whom in a moment creates play -
If he's wearing his hair-tie that day, and dreads ain't in the
way.

Martin Spencer's one of two strikers, he plays the right-
hand side.
But every time he gets a shot, the ball will end up wide.

Abid Ali plays in left-back, he runs the phone shop up the
road.
He'll sprint for around three seconds, before Abid has soon
slowed.

Simon Newman is our right back, he's not too bad but
often misses training.
But his general stamina is withering, and the manager is
complaining.

Janaka singh he plays left-centre mid, the hardest worker
of the team.
He's the one that often gets the ball, but don't always
tackle clean.

Jack Murphy plays right-centre back, it's true folk would be
lying,
if they said he didn't scare a bit, he'd send everyone flying.

We'v got Daniel Ştefănescu, whom plays on the right wing.
The fastest player on the team, but barely does a thing.

Michael Watson plays left-centre forward, but don't score
much at all.
Because he thinks that he's Ronaldo, and rarely once
passes the ball.

Nathan Gouth is our sub keeper,
he's only now just turned eighteen.
They reckon by next season,
he'll be the main one on our team.

Gavin Stuart, Tony Day, and Leroy Jackson-Jones,
can often be seen on the bench, checking Facebook on
their phones.

Mickey Parker is the manager,
And he sometimes turns up pissed.

He's even turned up to some games to find that they've
been missed.

The next week we have the FA cup, at Thonnington
Athletic.
Mickey said if they don't take this chance, then they'll
surely regret it.

"Come on lads! Let's do this thing!" Mickey to them said.
"Join me in staying sober all week, and swapping to brown
bread."

Saturday came, they won the game,
one-nil the final score.
They anticipated whilst they waited, for the FA cup draw.

The next match that they were to play, away at Hillston
United,
was one that they were to surely not win.
Until Francis Robinson ran, onto Clarke's curling corner,
for a last-minute diving header that went in.

The lads did celebrate on that Saturday night, and again
waited for the next draw.
They've only just gone and beat the Metropolitan Police!
And then just done a right number on York!

Leatheton's just made history, for this unknown little club.
The furthest that we've ever been, in the FA cup.
If we can somehow win the next game, we'll make it to the
first main round.
And who knows then what from there, we could do this
town proud.

Don't give us Barnet or Southport, and please not Torquay
United.
With a home draw against Hornchurch, the Leatheton Lads
had got excited.
They knew they still had to play well, and it wouldn't be
easy.
Michael Watson's only scored a hat-trick!
And we've won the game four-three!

It's the first time in our history, that we've got to the main
first round.
But surely this trip is over, when we go to Yeovil Town.
We held them to a nil-nil draw, and played quite well that
day.
And only gone and won one-nil, when we played the
replay!

They've all now cut down on their drinking, except for
those that do not drink.
But the dream is almost over now, everybody thinks.
"We've done so well to get this far, you all should be
proud and smile.
Don't feel bad if we get thrashed, by Plymouth Argyle."

We're losing by the second half, the score is now one-nil.
We're sixty-seven minutes in, only two shots we've had
still.
Then Clarke steps up for a free kick, looks like he's hoofed
it far.
But what a lob! In off the keeper, a rebound off the bar!

And on the eighty-second minute, Janaka Singh had then
ran through,
with one mighty dribble, and passed it to Ştefănescu.
He's right on the edge of the box, and Martin Spencer's
free.
But their defender pushes him.
It's a penalty!

Michael Watson steps to take it,
and you can see it means a lot.
He then kisses his closed fist,
and kicks the ball from the spot.
The keeper's chosen to go right,
slow-motion - eyes lock on.
Right down the centre, in the net,
the score is now two-one!

Plymouth go all-out-attack,
but Leatheton hold the ball.
*"We are the Leatheton United,
And we'll take on you all!"*

The third round of the FA cup, the whole town watches
the draw.
It will be the biggest ever sports event, that Leatheton's
seen before.
It's a home draw, and so we wait, for the next ball to be
drawn and there's nerves.
And then comes our fate, as they draw out an eight, which
means that we're going to play Spurs.

Just as expected, Leatheton were hammered,
but everyone in town had a great day.
The score seven-nil, but all of the town still,
will remember when Spurs came to play.

Jolly Jane and Sylvie

Jolly Jane and Sylvie, are always sat outside the café,
every Monday afternoon and on every market day.

Jolly Jane's big purple hat puts smiles on people's faces.
But she's not once been to the races, despite the way she
looks.

Jolly Jane and Sylvie will sit and watch the world go by.
And Jolly Jane will always say hi, if she catches your eye.

When they were both much younger, they danced the
Can-can in the town.
Back in the day they worked together, before the factory
had closed down.

Jolly Jane's husband was Eugene, Sylvie's husband -Jack,
But now have both since passed away, over ten years
back.
And every time that Jolly Jane, see's someone begging in
the street.
She'll always buy them a hot drink, and a pasty to eat.

They sit and chat there all day long, until ten-past-three.
And then both make their way home, up on the Birchtree.

When someone saw old Percy

Inside the big supermarket, where they had a café,
only two were in there eating, on a Wednesday rainy day.

The lady that worked in there, whom was counting up the
till,
went and got the kitchen mop, to clean up a spill.

Something had then touched her ear, she'd presumed that
it was flies.
And something then had tapped her shoulder, the lady
seemed surprised.

She turned around to see if there was someone right
behind.
But no-one was stood near her, it soon played on her
mind.

She looked to the far end of the room, where one young
man was sat.
And just a few tables away from her was an old man with a
flat cap.
Sipping on his strong tea, he's thinking and looking down.
"Hmm" she said before then turning back around.

The young man had then looked over, to the old man with
his tea.
Seen him put in another sugar, the sachet's now empty.
He rolls the sachet in his fingers, makes it into a ball.
Flicks it -missing her by an inch, it bounces off the wall.

The young man he tried hard not to laugh, the lady said
"What's that?"
The old man acted completely oblivious, with his head
down as he'd sat.

The children's home

Up at the top of St Peters Road, a set of conifers will hide,
the entrance of the children's home, that has eight kids
inside.
There's Justin, Sarah, Alfie, Robert, Crystal, Diane, Jax.
And Shane has gone to see his Mum, in three days he'll
come back.

One day there were three youngsters, inside of the home's
car.
On their way to then go to, the next town's cinema.
The two staff had just quickly gone, to search for their lost
keys.
"Has someone took them once again?
If you have then give them please!"

But no-one had taken the car keys, the staff were soon to
see.
But where they had parked up the car, the parking space
was free.
They heard some voices shouting loud, the staff ran up the
street.
Robert, Diane and Jax jumped out, but Alfie's in the driving
seat.

The car is rolling down the road, he knows of his mistake -
after thinking it was funny, to let off the handbrake.

And push the car on to the road, and send it rolling down.
But now he's hit a parked up car, and feels like a right clown.

The owner then came rushing out, and then soon called the police.
"We're bloody sick of this kids-home, and we all just want some peace."
They had complained to the Leatheton Gazette, of their frustrating pain.
But half of the stories weren't the full truth, and the kid's home often gets the blame.

They had started a petition, and wrote to their MP.
The total people that had signed it were no more than twenty-three.
It was obvious the neighbours there, were kicking up a rage.
"Children's home gang trouble" was the headline of the front page.

They'd written in the article so much that wasn't true.
Such as burglaries and break-ins, and drug dealing from there too.
A social worker called Linda said "Look this just ain't right.
We've got to show people the truth, and put up a good fight."

So then she hired the Rugby club, for a whole Saturday.
Laid on some entertainment, and put on a big buffet.
Invited all the local neighbours, to meet the kids living at the home.

It was the first time ever in this town, a glimpse of their
lives was shown.

The neighbours had soon come to learn, the stories from
in care.
And the feelings of abandonment and the trauma in some
there.
Abid Ali offered jobs, fixing phones once they'd turned
sixteen.
Diane's been offered to try out for the young women's
rugby team.

The day went on from ten up until six, a refreshing day in
Leatheton for sure.
Now Robert, Sarah and Jax have all found local foster
homes,
and the petition doesn't exist anymore.

The old man up the mountain

"Oh no Derry!" said his owner whilst being sat looking out
of her front window,
watching Derry chase a cat.

He's off again, got through the gate, the cat then quickly
fled,
up on to a wooden fence, then onto a coal shed.

He growls and barks up at the cat, which now looks smugly
down.
Then out comes Irene their neighbour, in slippers and a
dressing gown.

Derry makes a run for it, down an alleyway.
Runs through a set of garages, the neighbours out there
turn their heads.

Across the road, into the shop, before being chased back
out.
Then he wanders down folks garden paths, having a sniff
about.

And at the top of Jerome Street, Derry had then seen,
an old man walking his German Shepherd, which was now
fourteen.

The old man was called David Jones, and Lola his dog's
name.
Derry he went running up, to go and play a game.

But Lola being the aged she was, was too tired to play.
But David weren't the type of man to chase Derry away.

He patted Derry, then he looked at the name-tag Derry
wore,
then gave Derry a dog treat, before giving him two more.

Unknown to all the local kids, David used to be well-
known.
When he was weightlifting champion many years ago,
before he'd broke some bones.
You'd never guess it from his frame, but in his eyes you'll
see,
he's full of beans, a gentleman, and truly is friendly.

At sixty-nine you'd never guess, he looks more like forty-
four.
Every day he does his pull-ups, and his press-ups on the
floor.

And almost every Christmas day, David and Lola climb a
mountain top.

But now that Lola's getting old, at some point before they
stop.

And if you were to make him dinner, you should ask him
what he wants to eat.
Because it's now been over forty years, since David last ate
meat.

Leatheton's homeless hostel

Leatheton once had two homeless hostels, but now it just
has one.
Just like in the surrounding towns, most have closed down
and gone.

The only place that we've got here, if you're lucky to get
in,
is a hostel called *'Leatheton Chances'*, it's full of heroin.

The landlord has brought up half of the street,
but the look of it's quite bleak.
Even though he gets two hundred pounds for every room
a week.

It seems he's found a loophole, an easy way he can extort,
by claiming extra benefits, for personal support.

He's taking half of people's giro, in the name that they'll
get fed.
But they're all living off cheese sandwiches, which are
made with dry white bread.

Sometimes people get referred, and stay in there one
night,
before leaving the next morning, and saying "Thanks but
I'm alright."

The thickest smell of heroin, enough to make you sick.
You can be outside for hours, and still the smell on you will stick.
There's no place to cook your own food there, and after a report,
the trading standards and the landlord have been in and out of court.

But despite people's best efforts, no change at all yet has incurred,
because the landlord's mate works for the council, and can put in a good word.
Whether it's a funny handshake, or because of a surname,
the incompetence and corruption, plays out all the same.

Is this really Leatheton's future? Is this all our young people have?
And what about the hurting folk, that need a second chance?

It seems the more money that the landlord gets, the more this place gets nuts.
Please give us back our services, and stop these bloody cuts!

Come Dine With Me

Today we are in Leatheton, where five local contestants,
have a chance of winning a thousand pounds grand prize.
No-one knows until they get there, of whom else is taking
part.
But in the end it turns out that there's three women and
two guys.

First to host their dinner party, is a woman called Amita.
She uses her mum's recipe for a posh curry with posh
pitta.
The dress code there is Bollywood, and she does a belly
dance.
It seemed Amita has success, and is in with a chance.

They loved her starters and desert. They thought that her
home-made Lassi was heaven.
Amita's started off quite well, with a score of twenty-
seventy.

Next up it is Andrew's night, and he will make his own ice
cream.
It's written on his menu that 'In Ibiza' is the theme.
His garlic prawns still had their poop, his Paella turned to
gunk.
But only one of them had noticed, because all of them
were drunk.

He's put some whisky in the ice cream, and poured some
vodka shots,
His kitchen's piling up now,
with a mountain of big pots.

The others get into their cabs, and give Andrew their
score.
But Amita is still in the lead, Andrew's got twenty-four.

The next evening is Charlie's night. The main course is a
hearty stew.
And he's gone and called his starter –
'A mushroom with a view'.

They all loved his chocolate fudge cake, but they thought
his food was bland.
They all then had a little knees-up, when he played with
his brass-band.

Charlie's feeling confident, but despite all his tricks.
Amita is still in the lead, Charlie's got twenty-six.

The next night it's Swedish Helga, and the menu they
examine -
to see that she is going to make, 'posh eggs with smoked
salmon'.
No-one had guessed what 'posh eggs' meant, or if they
would be liking,
But they all chuckled when they saw – that her theme
night was 'Viking'.

She's made a fruity sponge cake and custard, with
cinnamon and nutmeg spice.
Despite her 'posh eggs' being simply basic, they thought
that it all had worked nice.

The Viking hats and fancy dress, had indeed caused some
cheer.
And then they all finished the night off, with a huge jug
each of beer.

Got into their taxi cabs, scorecards once again.
It seems Helga could do quite well, as she's just got a ten.
They all seem merry and with big smiles, it's time to give
their score.
And Helga is now in the lead, with a whopping thirty-four.

The next contestant Sarah-May, really must enhance,
on Helga's night, if she is to be in with a winning chance.
She's hoping that her posh menu, will make some pleasing
faces,
with her canapés and oysters, and her theme is 'At the
races'.

But she's been feeling quite anxious, and everyone can
tell.
It weren't until they ate desert, that she came out of her
shell.
But by the end they were all laughing, and all though the
food was great -
Sarah-May could have done much worse, with a final score
of twenty-eight.

So Helga is the prize winner, with her evening and her grub.
And when it came out on the telly, they put it on inside the pub.

Supershelf

Most of Leatheton had been quite excited when they had
found out,
that Supershelf were going to build a big warehouse in the
town.

"We'll have more jobs back in this place" some people
would shout.
But none of them were to foresee, the way it is there now.

They hardly get a single break, every single second timed.
Now you must stay in rigid order, and you must run to this
clock.
On your way out they'll scan you now, and treat you like
you've done a crime.
It seems this company is making our people a laughing
stock.

Except that it's not funny, when you zoom the camera out.
And see the man that's got no money, nor does he have
spare time.
And now he sooths himself with alcohol, to try and make
sense of it all.
He's a man that should be living in his prime.

Leatheton festival

It's Leatheton summer festival and everyone's in town.
We've never had one like this here, until three years ago.
But Big Jimmy from the marketplace has now brought one of the cafés.
Now on the stage are two musicians, and both are playing the banjo.

They've set up a big blank white wall, and there's a sign next to it says -
'If you want to do Graffiti – then you're welcome here's a space'.
And people have now set up stalls, raising money for hospitals.
There's handmade-wares, there's artists work and one stall that sells cakes.

And what starts off being fifteen folk, within an hour is eighty-four,
as the people in the town stop and watch all the bands play.
In the corner there's a Portaloo, and a magician passing through the crowd of people, doing tricks and leaving them in awe.

By midday the town is packed, the party now is in full
swing,
The word has spread through Facebook, Instagram and
Whatsapp.

And now the market square is rockin, with some really
nice Roots-Reggae.
And a local lad called Tom joins in to freestyle his own rap.

A lovely day, a great success, with people now feeling
refreshed.
It's nice to have something like this, in our Leatheton here.
A big thank you to all those involved, for helping Leatheton
show its soul.
And let's hope we get together, and do this again next
year.

THE END

Dedications

As some of you know, I've got a new poetry project called *'This Is Leatheton'* and have released the first book of it called *'Welcome To Leatheton'.*

I'd like to say a special thanks to everyone that inspired some of the characters from the book including -

For the poem 'Adam The Estate Agent' - All of the homeless young women living on the streets and long-term homelessness. Massive love to you tough souls.

For the poem 'Dedicated Caroline' - An actual dedicated soul called Caroline whom resided in a squat near Brick Lane, East London with us many memories ago. Likely departed and if so a true legend.

For the poem 'Jimmy-Jean the busker' - In memory of Johnny Walker 1980 - 2018, a national revolutionary fighter for buskers rights.

For the poem 'Sergeant Walter' - An odd bloke that went out of his way to poison people against me. Not only is quite toxic but also makes life hell for women he woos into thinking he is a soldier.

For the poem 'The Time Leatheton Got Snowed In' , a big shout out to Rob and all my other friends from the squat in Brighton. Great times.

For the poem 'Don The Champ' - Some bloke in North London the bus that I was on drove past.

For the poem 'Leatheton Folklore' - The town of Rugeley in Staffordshire and 'The Bloody Steps'.

For the poem 'CattleMarket Lane' - All of those campaigning against the rise in betting shops and roulette machines on Britain's high streets.

For the poem 'The week the gypsies came to town' - Sarah, a good soul.

For the poem 'Young Rebel' - Rory, a lad with open eyes and righteous vision.

For the poem 'When someone saw Old Percy' - An actual old man that cracked me up in Morrison's supermarket cafe in Rugeley, Staffordshire.

For the poem 'The Children's home' - Unknown to the public, yet wide among children in care, care leavers and social workers - the stigma and hateful vibes towards young people living in children's homes is very real. You didn't even get to know the young people that you were all complaining about. More unity is needed, we are all human beings.

For the poem 'The old man up the mountain' - I think his name was Mark.

For the poem 'Leatheton festival' - To Kerst, Jayne, Neil, Johnny, Tracey, Bob and everyone else ;)

MASSIVE LOVE TO ALL OF UM, EVEN SERGEANT WALTER, I'VE HAD WORSE.

In memory of Phil
1978 - 2019

About the author

Ben Westwood is a musician, writer, poet and campaigner.

He released his debut book 'Poems From a Runaway – A True Story' in 2017.
It's a sixty-story 'novel-in-verse' and his accounts of going through childhood and being a runaway from ten years old, and from twelve sleeping rough in London – as well as going through the care system.

He uses his story to raise awareness of life in foster care, children's homes, and on the streets as well as helping to give more insight to those working with young people and families, as well as the general public.

You can find it on Amazon and
Benwestwooduk.blogspot.co.uk

Find me on Twitter at @PoemsFaRunaway

#ThisIsLeatheton

Huge thank you to Neil Paterson for the brilliant doodles.

Neil Paterson is an artist and illustrator adept at many different styles including traditional, pencil, watercolour, oils, digital and computer generated images.
He is currently working on a self-promotional series of paintings inspired by a local beauty spot 'Cannock Chase' called 'Spirits of the Chase'
Twitter @NeilPaterson @spiritsofthechase
instagram: neopaterson
facebook.com/spiritsofthechase
www.lynniel.com

Thanks for reading.

Printed in Great Britain
by Amazon

21610058R00079